THE LEOPARD LICKS ITS SPOTS

The Leopard Licks its Spots

Published by Kalenga Augustine Mulenga

Johannesburg, South Africa

augustine@kamulenga.com

ISBN 978-0-620-91000-2

2 4 6 8 10 9 7 5 3 1

Publication facilitation Boutique Books

Printed in South Africa by Bidvest Data

By K.A. Mulenga

Chuck the Cheetah

David, the great king

Donk and the Stubborn Donkeys

Drew, the Dragon

Elaine the Elephant

Four seasons in one day

Harry the Honest Horse

Imbwa, the Story Of the Dog and His Harsh Master

Joe Finds His Way Home

Max the Gorilla

Never Give Up

Pete the Panda

Polly the Polecat

Robbie the Raven and Debbie the Dove

Spike and Spud , the Spaceboys

Susie Strickland, Sizzling Striker

The Leopard Licks Its Spots

The Lion and the Impala

The Weaver Birds

Uni the Unicorn

Will and His Best Friend Whale

Leroy, the Leopard, lived in the Savannah with his family: Daddy Leopard, Mummy Leopard and Grandpa Leopard.

Grandpa Leopard was the chief. He was the oldest and wisest of all the leopards in the Savannah.

Leroy had a best friend. His name was Lapa. Lapa was the best friend any leopard could have. Leroy and Lapa would play in the grass, climb in the trees and enjoy the beautiful Savannah every day.

One day, Leroy and Lapa saw one of the other leopards stealing meat from a tree. It was Loopey, also known as Loopey the Lonely. This was because he was always alone, and he had no friends or family.

The meat belonged to Lapa's mother, she had left it there for the family to eat later.

Leroy and Lapa went straight to Grandpa Leopard to report what they had seen.

"I HEREBY CALL A MEETING OF THE LEOPARDS," Grandpa Leopard said in his booming voice. All the leopards gathered around and waited to hear what Grandpa Leopard had to say.

"YOU HAVE BEEN ACCUSED OF STEALING MEAT THAT DID NOT BELONG TO YOU," he said pointing at the thief. "Leroy and Lapa saw you taking the meat, so you cannot defend yourself. You are hereby banished to the other side of the Savannah for a week!" he pronounced with authority.

Off went the thief, embarrassed and ashamed.

“You are so wise, Grandpa,” said Leroy.

“A LEOPARD LICKS BOTH IT’S WHITE AND BLACK SPOTS”, Grandpa said.

“You always say that after pronouncing judgement, Grandpa. What does it mean?” Leroy asked.

“You will learn one day, my boy. Now go and play, I need to rest,” Grandpa said with a big yawn.

A week later, Leroy and Lapa were playing in the Savannah as usual. They noticed some meat on the ground, and they wondered whose it was.

“I do not think anyone owns this meat,” Lapa said.

“Neither do I,” said Leroy.

“I am hungry,” Lapa said licking his lips, “so, are we agreed, Leroy?

“Come on. No one is watching, so let us dig in,” said Leroy.

“Hey, you! Leopards. You are eating my meat,” came a shout from the other side.

It was the thief from last week!, “Come on. I am taking you both to Grandpa Leopard!” said the thief.

“WHAT HAVE THESE BOYS DONE?” Grandpa Leopard asked in his big, booming voice.

“They ate my meat without asking me!” said the thief.

“You were seen taking the meat, Leroy and Lapa. So, you cannot defend yourselves. You are both banished to the other side of the Savannah for a week!” he pronounced with authority.

“But, I am your grandson,” cried Leroy.

“A LEOPARD LICKS BOTH IT’S WHITE AND BLACK SPOTS,” Grandpa said.

“You always say that after pronouncing judgement, Grandpa, even to me and Lapa. Please tell me, what does it mean?”

“It means justice should be served fairly to all those in power and, even though you are my grandson, you cannot get special treatment when you have done wrong!” Grandpa said.

“You are so wise, Grandpa,” said Leroy.

Thank you for reading The Leopard Licks Its Spots, I hope you enjoyed it! Please let K.A. Mulenga know about what you thought about the book by leaving a short review on Amazon, it will help other parents and children find the story. (If you're under 13, ask a grown up to help you)

Top Tip: Be sure not to give away any of the story's secrets!